The Photo Book

Story by Beverley Randell
Illustrations by Serena Geddes

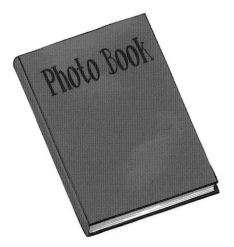

Here is the photo book.

Mom   Dad

Kate

James

Nick

Mom is in the book.

Mom

Dad is in the book.

Dad

James is in the book.

Here is James.

James

Nicola

Nick

Kate is in the book.

Here is Kate.

Dad
Kate
James
Nicola
Nick

Nick is in the book.

Here is Nick.

Mom Dad Kate James Nick Nicola

Here is Teddy.

Teddy is in the book, too.

Mom　　Dad

Kate　　James

Nick　　Teddy